Rhinos Don't Eat Pancakes

Written by Anna Kemp   Illustrated by Sara Ogilvie

A Paula Wiseman Book
Simon & Schuster Books for Young Readers
New York   London   Toronto   Sydney   New Delhi

For Monty, with love—A. K.

For Avril and Robert
(never too busy to listen)—S. O.

SIMON & SCHUSTER BOOKS FOR YOUNG READERS

An imprint of Simon & Schuster Children's Publishing Division

1230 Avenue of the Americas, New York, New York 10020

Originally published in 2011 in Great Britain by Simon & Schuster UK Ltd.

First US edition 2015

For information about special discounts for bulk purchases, please contact Simon & Schuster

Special Sales at 1-866-506-1949 or business@simonandschuster.com.

The Simon & Schuster Speakers Bureau can bring authors to your live event. For more information or to book an event, contact

the Simon & Schuster Speakers Bureau at 1-866-248-3049 or visit our website at www.simonspeakers.com.

Book design by Tom Daly

The text for this book is set in Horley Old Style MT Std.

The illustrations for this book are rendered in pencil, pastel, ink, paint, monoprint, as well as digitally.

Manufactured in China

0215 SCP

2   4   6   8   10   9   7   5   3   1

CIP data for this book is available from the Library of Congress.

ISBN 978-1-4814-3845-2

ISBN 978-1-4814-3850-6 (eBook)

Do you ever get the feeling that your mom and dad aren't listening to a word you say?

You do? Then you are just like Daisy. Her mom and dad never listen. Daisy could tell them that their hair was on fire or that the dog had eaten the mailman, but they would just nod and say, "That's nice, dear," or "Tell your gran," or "Can't you see I'm on the phone?"

So when one day Daisy had something really important to say, guess what?

NOBODY LISTENED.

So this is what happened . . .

Daisy was eating her breakfast when a big purple rhino strolled into the kitchen.

That's right,
a big purple rhino!

It was as big as a bus and as purple as a plum.

It was also hungry. So it took a chomp of Daisy's pancake and went upstairs.

"Mom! Mom!" Daisy called.
"There's a big—"

"Tell your dad," said Mom.
"He'll catch it in a mug and throw it out the window."

"Dad! Dad!" said Daisy.
"There's a big, there's a huge—"

"Shhh!" said Dad. "The spider can wait."

"It's not a spider!" Daisy shouted.
"It's a big purple RHINOCEROS!"

But, as usual, **NOBODY LISTENED.**

Meanwhile, the rhino made himself right at home.

Daisy saw him in the hall,

and glimpsed him in the yard.

She spied him in the bathroom.

But every time she tried to tell her parents, they'd say, "Shhhh! Daisy. Can't you see we're BUSY?"

Daisy's parents were busy all week.

So Daisy began to talk to the rhino instead.

Soon they became good friends.

They played ring toss, and made pizza together,
and the rhino tickled Daisy until she thought she'd burst.
But Daisy's parents didn't notice.

Until the pancakes ran out.

"Who ate all the pancakes?"
yelled Dad, looking straight at Daisy.

"It was the rhino," she said.

"Rhinos don't eat pancakes," said Dad.

"This one does!" cried Daisy. "I saw him in the kitchen."

"A rhino?" said Mom.

"In the kitchen?" said Dad.

"YES!" said Daisy. "Exactly!"

Mom and Dad roared with laughter.
"What next?" they hooted. "A shark in the toilet?
A polar bear in the fridge?"

"**THERE HE IS, LOOK!**" Daisy yelled.

But Mom and Dad were so busy laughing they didn't even notice.

"Come on, Rhino," said Daisy, "I've had enough of this."

The rhino tickled Daisy with his horn.
But she was far too glum to giggle.

"Mom and Dad never listen," she sighed. "They are always a million miles away."
The rhino sighed deeply through his big purple nostrils.

"I'm sorry, Rhino," said Daisy. "Your family is a million miles away too, isn't it?"

The rhino nodded and a lilac tear rolled down his cheek.

Poor Rhino.

That night Daisy sat up, thinking of ways to get the rhino back home to his family.

He was too heavy for a hot-air balloon,

and too big for Daisy's rubber dinghy.

She thought about lending him her bike, but the helmet would never fit.

The next morning, Mom and Dad had a surprise.
"We're taking you to the zoo!" said Mom. "So you can see
a REAL rhino."
"What do you think of that?" Dad grinned.

Daisy thought it was a stupid
idea when there was already
a perfectly good rhino sitting
on the sofa.

But she didn't say so.
What was the point?

NOBODY WOULD LISTEN.

At the zoo, Daisy saw yellow giraffes . . .

bright red parrots . . .

orange and black tigers, and grass-green snakes.

But she couldn't help thinking about her poor purple rhino.
"Hurry up, Daisy," said Mom. "The rhinos are this way."

But what was this?

"Cripes!" gasped Mom.

"Well, that explains the pancakes!" gasped Dad.

Mom, Dad, and Daisy rushed back home—
and guess what they saw when they got there?

That's right, the biggest,

purplest rhinoceros in town!

"What did I tell you?" Daisy said, grinning from ear to ear.

"I'm calling the zoo," said Mom.

The rhino looked startled.

"No!" said Daisy. "Not the zoo. He needs to get back
to his family. They are a million miles away."

"Well, we'd better get a move on," said Dad. "The next
flight to a Million Miles Away leaves this afternoon."

The rhino packed his suitcase while Daisy found his hat. Then they all pushed his big purple bottom into the back of the car . . .

and drove to the airport.

"I'll miss you," said Daisy as the rhino boarded the plane.
The rhino gave her a big purple hug. He would miss her, too.

Back at home, Daisy began to feel lonely again.
Who would listen to her now?

But little did she realize that everything was about to change.

"Tell us about the rhino, Daisy," said Mom.
"Yes," said Dad. "Tell us about that big, purple, pancake-eating rhino."

So Daisy told them about the ring toss and
the pizza and the tickles and guess what?

They listened and listened until she had completely run out of words.

IT WAS WONDERFUL.

"Is there anything else you'd like to tell us?"
asked Mom as she tucked Daisy into bed that night.

Daisy looked out onto the landing.

"No, that's all for now," said Daisy, smiling. "Night night!"

The pink polar bear would have to wait till tomorrow.